D1451809

Sarah first heard the noise on Tuesday.

"No more games now," her mom had said as she tucked her into bed.

But after she closed the door,

Sarah immediately grabbed her phone and flicked on TerraForm.

She was only 30 gems away from world six.

Then the noise caught her attention.

It sounded a bit like a BEEP. And a lot like a THUMP.
Then it came again. BEEP. THUMP. THEEP.

Sarah put her phone down and sat up.

That's when she saw it.

A creature made of glowing brown squares and pulsing red pixels.

Sitting on the edge of her bed.

BEEP. THEEP.

Sarah stared.

The creature looked a bit like a beaver,
but one that had come from a computer game.
It had a big flat tail and an inquisitive face.
"Are you real?" asked Sarah, leaning forward.
BEEP. The beaver looked at her. THEEP.

Sarah wanted to get back to her game.
Only 30 gems left to get.
She kept one eye on the beaver and reached for her phone.
"Don't do that!" the creature said.

"What?!" asked Sarah.
"The game!" said the beaver. It scratched at her comforter
and sat itself down. "Don't go back to the game."
"Why?" asked Sarah with a frown. "I only need 30 more gems."
"Humph," said the beaver. Then it THEEPed again.

The beaver pulled a pixelated stick out from under its feet.
Then some blocky leaves.
"What are you doing?" Sarah asked.
"Protecting you," replied the beaver.
Sarah tilted her head. "From what?"
"You!" the beaver said.

The beaver started to make a dam, right at the foot of Sarah's bed.
Made of computer graphic twigs and video game mud.
"I don't understand," said Sarah.
"You will," said the beaver.
Then it THEEPed again.

Five minutes later, the beaver finished its creation.
A huge pile of sticks and leaves stood at the end of Sarah's bed.
"OK, try now," the beaver said.
"Try what?" Sarah asked.
"Your game."

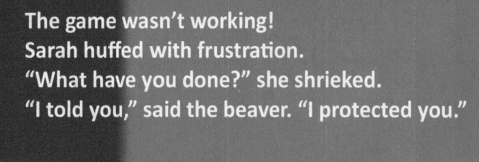

The game wasn't working!
Sarah huffed with frustration.
"What have you done?" she shrieked.
"I told you," said the beaver. "I protected you."

Sarah felt herself lose control.
She was going to have a tantrum.
"Make it work NOW!" she cried.
"Not until we've had a talk," said the beaver. "Follow me."
And it scurried into its dam.

Sarah looked at the mess at the end of her bed.
She leaned in closer and reached out to touch it.
And then she climbed inside.

"Where are we?" asked Sarah.
The inside of the dam was bright and noisy.
There were lots of BEEPS and THEEPS.
"This is the internet," said the beaver.
"I thought you liked it here."

"Over here is a big door that's easy to open," said the beaver.
"That's how I got into your room."
Sarah frowned. "It looks a bit broken."
"Yes, that's because your password is easy to guess,
and you've told too many people what it is."
Sarah's eyes widened with worry.
"Look, can you see how anyone could come in if they wanted to?"
Sarah nodded and her cheeks turned pink.
She felt a little embarrassed.

"What's this?" she asked, pointing to a big pile of junk in the corner.

"Oh, that's your malware," said the beaver.

"My what?"

"All that stuff you say 'yes' to that you don't really think about.
All the apps and software that sit on your phone without you realizing."

A creature popped its head up from the pile and grinned at Sarah.

She jumped.

"What's that?"

"He's called Mal, the Malware Fairy," the beaver replied,
"and he's not particularly nice."

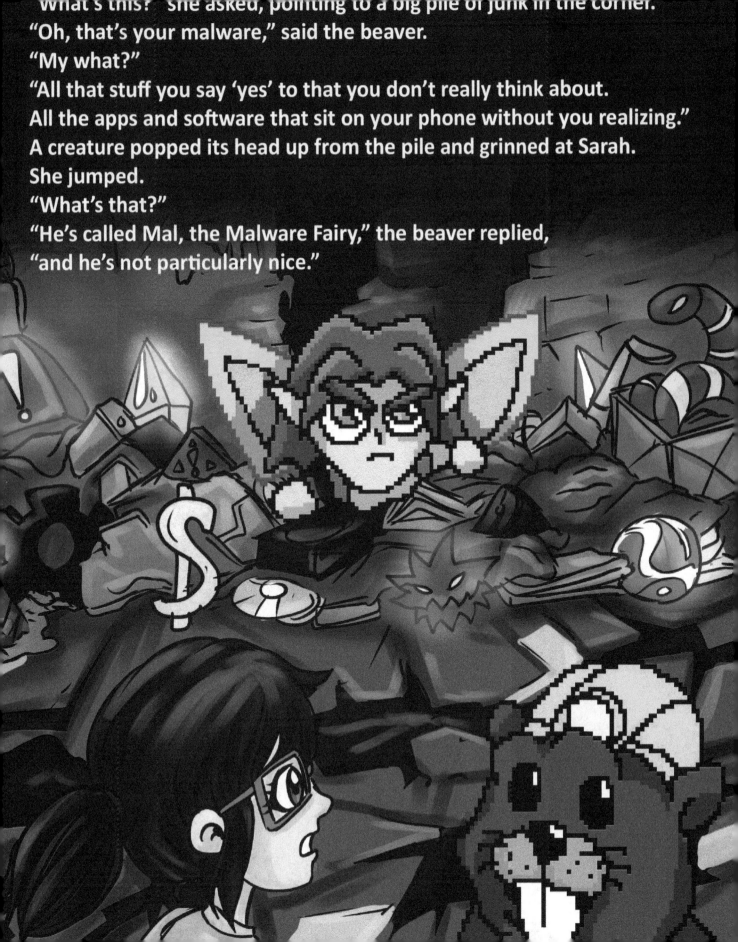

"I don't understand," said Sarah, "why is all this stuff here?"

"There's lots of stuff on the internet that's not good for you," said the beaver. "Oh, there's plenty that is fun, but you have to be careful."

Sarah's shoulders relaxed. "Oh, well there's nothing to worry about then, I'm always careful." The beaver shook its head. "You, Sarah, are not careful."

"I am!"

"Really?" asked the beaver, "then what's this?"

The beaver scurried off through a tunnel and Sarah followed.
They suddenly found themselves on top of a cloud.
"Look down!" said the beaver. Sarah gasped. "I can see my house!"
"Yup. You and everyone else who comes here."
"What do you mean?" asked Sarah.
"You know when something asks you about your location?
If it can track you?" Sarah nodded. "Yes."
"Well, you say 'yes', don't you?" "Umm…"
"Well, now everyone knows where you live."
Sarah's stomach twisted. "Everyone? Even that creature
from back there?" "Definitely him. Anyone who wants to know. Come on."

Sarah followed the beaver back into the dark dam.

"We're going to clean up!" said the beaver.

He handed Sarah a broom.

"Clean up?"

"Yup. Everything. We're going to sweep it all away."

He THEEPed.

"And then what?"

"Then you'll be safe," the beaver said with a smile.

The beaver helped Sarah sweep away the malware.
Each time Mal popped his head out,
Sarah bashed it with the broom. Eventually, the fairy ran away.

Together, Sarah and the beaver fixed her door.
"Pick a better password," said the beaver,
"something you'll remember that no one else will guess. And don't tell anyone."
"Even Mom and Dad?" asked Sarah.
"Just Mom and Dad," said the beaver. "They're there to protect you, too."

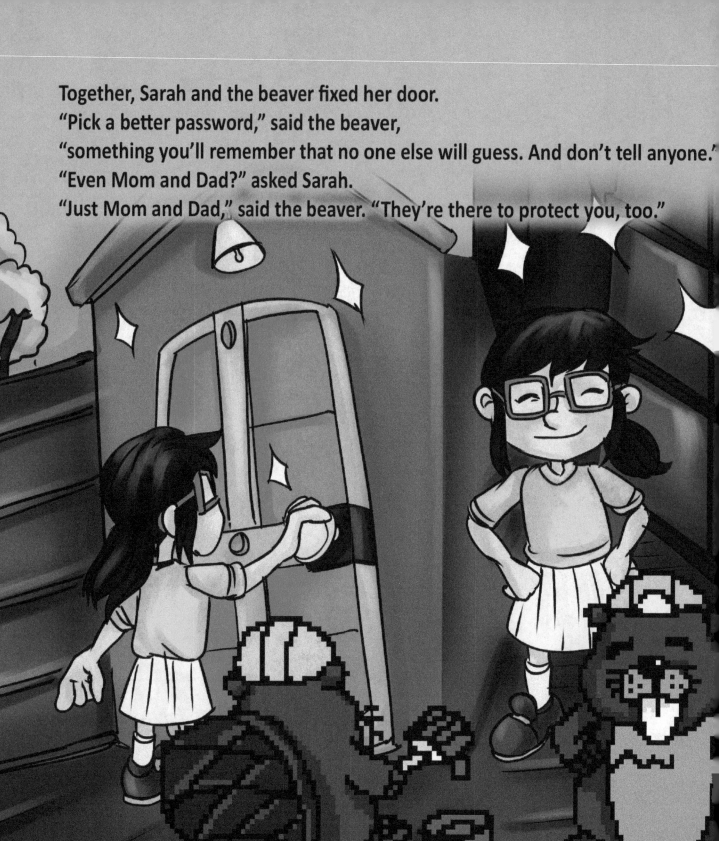

Sarah and the beaver blocked up the tunnel that led to her house.
"There, now no one will be able to see where you live either,"
said the beaver, smiling.

Sarah crawled out of the dam and back onto her bed.
There, sitting on her pillow, was Mal.
"Beaver!" Sarah squealed, pointing at the fairy.
The fairy grinned and picked up her phone.
"Oh no!" the beaver exclaimed. "Were we too late?"

The Malware Fairy grinned and started pressing
the buttons on her phone.
The beaver jumped into the air and plummeted
with a THEEP on Sarah's pillow.
Mal bounced, tumbled, and crashed. Right onto Sarah's foot.

Sarah grabbed at Mal.
"Gimme my phone!" she said.
The fairy held on tightly, but Sarah was stronger.
With a furious tug, she pulled him free and threw him into the dam.
Quickly, the beaver pulled some more sticks and leaves together,
sealing the hole.

"He's not getting out now," said the beaver. "You promise?"
"That's a sturdy dam," the beaver assured.
"A proper firewall. It'll protect you from all the nasty things
on the internet - as long as you take care yourself."
"Oh, I will!" Sarah looked at her phone.
"Does that mean I shouldn't play TerraForm anymore?"
The beaver smiled. "No, you can still play your game,
 just be careful about what you say yes to." Sarah nodded.

Sarah only needed 30 gems to reach world six, but she turned off her phone and put it on the bedside table.

"I think I should go to sleep, now," she said with a yawn.

"The game can wait."

"It definitely can," the beaver agreed. "Sleep is much more important."

"Will you be here when I wake up?" Sarah asked.

"No," said the beaver, shaking his head. "I've got other dams to build. You're not the only little girl who doesn't know enough about cybersecurity." He smiled. "But I'll be back to check on you."

"Promise?" asked Sarah.

"I promise," said the beaver.

In the morning, Sarah changed her background picture.
"Is that from your game?" asked Mom.
"Something like that," said Sarah. "You know, Mom,
I need to talk to you about cybersecurity..."

CPSIA information can be obtained
at www.ICGtesting.com
Printed in the USA
LVHW060359160622
721421LV00003B/5